JESSICA
THE STORM COLLECTION

AF111149

TEMPESTT

JESSICA

THE STORM COLLECTION

TEMPESTT

Jessica
The Storm Collection

Copyright © 2023 by Tempestt

Paperback ISBN: 978-1-63812-536-5
Hardback ISBN: 978-1-63812-681-2
Ebook ISBN: 978-1-63812-537-2

All rights reserved. No part in this book may be produced and transmitted in any form or by any means, electronic, or mechanical, including photocopying, recording, or by any information storage and retrieval system, without permission in writing from the copyright owner.

The views expressed in this work are solely those of the author and do not necessarily reflect the views of the publisher hereby disclaims any responsibility for them.

Published by Pen Culture Solutions   04/26/2023

Pen Culture Solutions
1-888-727-7204 (USA)
1-800-950-458 (Australia)
support@penculturesolutions.com

7 DAYS, THEN ....

CONTENTS

Chapter 1= Leaving 1

Chapter 2= Day 1 3

Chapter 3= Day 2 5

Chapter 4 = Day 3 6

Chapter 5 = Day 4 7

Chapter 6 = Day 5 8

Chapter 7= Day 6 9

Chapter 8 = Day 7 11

Chapter 9 = Leave or Stay 13

Chapter 10= The Talk With Mother And Her Siblings 15

Chapter 11 =The Gentleman Waited in the Lobby Till Breakfast was served 17

Chapter 12 = The Talk with Breakfast Man Dad 19

Chapter 13 =Bank Transfer 20

Chapter 14 = Jessica got a baby 22

Chapter 15 = Earl Back 24

Chapter 16= Return to Home for three days 26

Chapter 17= Day 1 At Home 28

Chapter 18 =Day 2 back Home 30

Chapter 19=Day 3 Back home 32

Chapter 20= On the way back home Jessica received good news ... 34

Chapter 21= There is a God 36

Chapter 22= Jessica moves to an Island with her family 38

Chapter 23= The uproar 40

Chapter 24 The call from the doctor 42

Chapter 25 The Baby 44

Chapter 26 Together forever 45

Chapter 27 What you going to do? 47

Dedication 48

Sneak Peak Of Jessica Book 2 Chapter 1 .... *49*

About Author: 51

Chapter 1= Leaving

Have you ever felt your identity gone? Left with no direction? Maybe like a piece of you is missing? When everything feels good but it's all a lie! Have you ever been betrayed by the ones you love? Don't know if you love or how to love? To be in love is a feeling that you have with someone. Have you made a connection that was built on a lie? Trust is hard to come by so when you have it, you must hold on to it and do what you have to do to remain in trust. But, trust is very tricky especially if you already don't trust the person. So it's already a lack of love. Broken love is no good, holding on to something you don't need , Can be hard to let go . Especially if it's familiar, you don't ever want to lose it. Change is hard to take on. Because having the same flow it allows you to know what is already expected. Being in a toxic cycle is hard to break. Especially if you don't know it's toxic. Because what's toxic to you could be normal to another. It causes you to overthink and can lead you into insanity. It makes it even harder when you are trying to let go. Then, when something good comes around, you don't know if it's good or if it's a show. Many sleepless nights, It's hard to find a complete balance. It's as if trouble always follows you. To sleep is to be at peace! Resting in peace sounds good but is it really good? Then, that's when you give up on sleep, what's next? Running off fumes, work is drowning, abusing alcohol, Maybe not agreeing with your family, Dealing with grief and love life is toxic or never boring, You become full but you haven't eaten yet. But it's all familiar; you don't want to break the chain. If you have stuck to a consistent plan and it's not working. Maybe it is time for a change.

A leap of faith to see where you will end. It's hurting but you feel like if you break away , It will kill you. Crying, and just hurting yourself , will not help it, only cause more harm. It is time for her to go and plan a 7 day vacation. 7 Days will save the mental abuse that's been in her head. The bruises from many different occasions, lies that have been told, drugs that she would say she would never use, and Her life is dealing with turmoil. She's happy so she think. Then she's upset, and crying. She's very moody and everyone is very needy. She has to smile even though she feels like crying. She says she loves you but she hates you too. But now she's in need. Pride dies down when it comes to one thing. But that soon builds back up. Because she continues to overthink instead of being around positive vibes ,she doesn't understand normal. Time after Time, she must get away and find peace. Where do you go when you want to just get away? Will she even be missed? How long will it take for someone to come find her? What if she has no plans but still gets in the car and drives. What if she goes somewhere she has been but she has no memories. She is running and she must breathe. "Drive , Drive away, find your peace , Leave everything and don't come back." But what about her family? Her siblings have been unlinked and one can never be joined again, But she is so close to all her siblings. Why don't they know she's hurting? Does she really walk around being weird smiling knowing that she is hurting? "Drive , Drive" The voices she hears keep telling her but she is scared to listen because that's a sign of insanity. "Make it worth your while!"

Chapter 2= DAY 1

Lost and alone she listened to that voice. It's time to grow up and figure things out.

To a place unknown, where she wouldn't know nobody. And nobody will know her!

She thinks it is a plan. A great one at that. "Less stress will ease the mind." The voice said.

Where no one would know her , She would be able to run away! This wouldn't be the first time. She runs away from all her problems. But, she had to leave this time for real. Earl really did it this time. She needed peace. But trying to find companionship so she won't be alone. But she wants to be alone. Because to love Earl is just like being alone. But he surely is all she knows. She found out it was something else. Maybe it wasn't companionship she needed, it was maybe happiness. Crossing the lines, state to state gone on 'em! Entering a New State made her so small. Looking for directions to navigate because GPS doesn't locate what she is trying to find. She doesn't know what she is trying to find. Maybe it's what! Maybe it's who! Maybe it's them! "Change the scene!" "Don't be afraid!" "We are still in the country right?" She's so sheltered. It's the language but they look like me. Her name hasn't been mentioned yet because she doesn't even know who she is. Or who she will be! Now she is okay! She eats and fuels the car, now she's searching for a hotel for about a week. She feels that's all the peace she needs away from home. She plans to return but, at this moment, it's too much. She sees water. To the beach she goes. She hears the beach is much more peaceful.

She is used to land. When only land and trees surround you, it's the swimming pool. Maybe a lake to fish. Very small but its home and her heart is still there. "The little bit she has!" Scared of change but where she went was a major change. "You on to something!" She is now ready to go back to the hotel. The first night she thought it was peace. But, passing the front desk she noticed a bar not to mention the mini shots upon arrival. She enjoyed the bar and was escorted upstairs. She didn't know who it was but at that moment she was at peace. It's a change so she feels it's safe. She's relieved and entered her room alone. She enjoyed that night.

Chapter 3= Day 2

She wakes up to a complimentary wakeup call from the hotel's receptionist, telling her about "the breakfast buffet." She figures it's time to get up and start her day. No plans, no thoughts, and the phone left on don't bother me with undisturbed music and GPS. She stops down stairs, the same escort from last night greets her with her favorite bacon and cheese sandwich cut down the middle. She was confused. So she thought, Maybe they eat like this too. So, she's looking around for the buffet and it's not there. The food she sees is not equivalent to her favorite. Maybe it's too late, she didn't get up as fast as she thought she did. "This has to be brunch!" But the clock is set at 9:00 am. She decided to go on about her day. Still away from what she knows. Missed calls and text messages. She still went about her day. Not letting anyone or drama mess up her day. " What about your loved ones , at least call your mom and siblings!" But she doesn't do any of that. Maybe she will switch her number? She really doesn't want to do that! Because that may make them gone forever. It's an attachment that she just doesn't want to give up! She went to the mall that was nearby and went to look around her surroundings. She needed to at least know where she was. Or what she was by. She enjoyed her day and was at peace. She needed to pinch herself to make sure it was real. "It has really been a stress free day and she is smiling ear to ear and it's a smile from happiness to not be stressed out!

Chapter 4 = Day 3

It was another phone call that morning that woke her up. This was the most consistent thing in her life right now. Same breakfast sandwich, she felt as if someone was watching over her. "A good day to go to the beach." Wind blowing and she was ready to go, but as she was getting in her car, her past came back. Earl stopped the door. She was surprised. But it was a weird surprise. She was happy that she saw someone she knew but it had to be Earl. How did he know where she was? He was a reason she decided to get away. Earl caused a scene. She was so embarrassed, but the commotion caused others to surround her, and quickly the man from the hotel saved her from her troubles. They called authorities! She left after the police came and they took Earl away. After so much commotion she decided to go back up to her room. On the way to the room she decided to have a drink or drinks. She went back to her room, with a note of a new hotel that was across the city but it was downtown. With roses and gift cards. The new room was paid for 7 days. "It was a whole reset! In the envelope was a full refund for $1500. She left and went no questions asked. It was different because she enjoyed her time. It was as if she was in the same place just moved across town. She decided to stay in that night. The rest was unmatched. She's only resting in peace and she's alive. She had a new feeling about resting in peace.

Chapter 5 = Day 4

It's a new day! She's feeling refreshed. She received a complimentary call again. Downstairs for breakfast, the same man was standing there with her favorite breakfast sandwich and OJ. She didn't think nothing of it, she enjoyed her breakfast and afterwards she found a $500 gift card, with a note on her table, "Thanks for sharing time here at the resorts." She again didn't think nothing of it. She's up $2000, why not enjoy the day. It was earlier, she decided to go on a cruise. $500 for a 2 day cruise. She says why not. She left her phone, turned off at the hotel so she wouldn't have no location on. She didn't bring any clothes, only the reward money and her passport. Getting aboard it was a tall gentleman that caught her attention. She had caught his attention. Her eyes lit up. It was like having your first High. It was love at first sight. "He was fine, looking like he speak 20 languages." Still not in reality, she had been through so much she decided to let her guard down and enjoy herself. She enjoyed every inch of the boat. She went in all the stores and every relaxed setting. Then she went in the store and scanned her boat ID and they asked if you would like to use your boat perks. Instantly her face lit up she was interested to know the amount. $3500 have been added with $250 boat perks. Still holding on to her money she used all the boat perks.

Still thinking nothing other than blessed she doesn't question how she's getting all this money but she is overfilled. She's happy and believes it's a relief of healing.

Chapter 6 = Day 5

A note canceled the trip early. Finally the next day the gentleman leaves her early in the morning. She thought to herself, "Dang he just left like that, we leave in 6 Hrs." Still over thinking she received a knock at the door. It was him! 150 count roses red and white. Breakfast and more, she never been surprised before. This was very unfamiliar, now she has all this stuff but she can't take them home. She thought it was too much, the gentleman ordered movers to carry her stuff back to any location that was given to them. She is surprised he's not asking for contact information and trying to leave. As she says goodbye she's just wondering if they will ever meet again. She arrives back to the hotel she was transferred too and noticed she had to stop the movers from putting in her stuff inside the room. The whole room had been trashed. Her phone was broken. She was devastated she didn't know what to do. Instantly she looks around and see the breakfast man who always have her breakfast. She quickly asks, "what's happening," he's there and he said "He has seen the camera footage and they have extended her stay to 2 weeks in the presidential suite. Where she will be the only one on the floor. Still not thinking nothing but glad the problems over. Now that all her old stuff was damage she decided to go a night without the technology. She decided to unpack in the morning and go to bed. But she fell asleep and was not able to finish. "Tomorrow will be a better day!" Still in positive spirits she remembers what she saw,and who she saw.

Chapter 7= Day 6

Waking up to the morning call. She decided to skip breakfast to go through her things and unpack. As she unpack she remembers she needs to get a phone today. She continues to unpack to notice a new phone in the box. She was surprised as she opened the phone and as soon as she opened it. There were missed calls and text messages. A knock at her door, it made her start smiling from ear to ear. Because she doesn't know what to expect. She looked out to see a cart with breakfast and she was astonished. Excitement filled the room. Phone starts ringing and she answers the unknown number. She remembered the voice. "Here goes that smile again." It was the gentleman she had a good time with. Still she thinks nothing of it. They decided to meet up, as she leaving the room the same man from the last hotel at the desk, "Did you enjoy your food?" She replied, "Yes." Still just excited she left to enjoy her date. New to dating, She's 27 but never been on a date. She has had one relationship and nothing or no one has ever made her feel this way. She didn't know how to act. Didn't know if arms were on table or off table. She wants plastic ware and plastic cups. She thought he would judge her but she continued to be herself. "May I have plastic utensils?" After dinner he wanted to take her to so many places. She didn't have tennis shoes and a chill outfit, so he took her to the mall to avoid going to the room. She changed into the new clothes, he even brought a duffel bag so her clothes wouldn't be all over the car. She enjoyed the date and they had a good time. Still looking for him to try to come over. She never felt affection without touching. It was all new to her so she went back to the presidential suite and decided to reach out to her friends from back home. She invited them to come down but they were all busy. "Now she's sad." It was a rejection feeling she had. The alone feeling because she didn't want to be alone but didn't want to be alone with the gentleman. She decided to come out of her comfort zone. She called the gentleman up and they talked all night long as if they had known each other forever. She started to get in her feelings because it's been a minute since she had that kind of attention. She even told him that tonight might be her last night but she already had paid for rooms and she only took a week off from work. He had a sense of understanding. So she was confused and thought he didn't like her.

Chapter 8 = Day 7

Today she woke up and she said, "I should really be getting back but she still had days remaining in the room. So far away no friend to have with her to really enjoy. But, maybe she's better off alone. She is learning how to be alone. She had to think of whether today is going to be the last day or will she leave. A knock at the door with roses this time a 48 count. With a letter attached," Dear My Long Lost Love, I'm sorry to come to you after all this time but, I know today was your time to leave. If you can stay longer, meet me downstairs. "She gets dressed quickly and she thinks it's the gentleman she met. But still confused because it could be Earl. "But he doesn't buy flowers,nor is he romantic enough." She walks down and sees the breakfast man. He asked to talk with her. She learns he is her father and he knew she would come to this spot. Her father used to bring her there all the time and the breakfast is what she would always get her. Eyes filled with tears because he needs to know if she is a match. Not because it's his daughter. He explains, "The drug and abuse he has been through. How so much pain and her mother didn't allow them to be together because of their personal issues. He asked, "May you get tested?" She didn't hesitate to say, "Yes". Now she was going to an appointment that was already scheduled. They run test and she was a match. She was so quick to answer because she knew it was for a DNA test. But, he was willing to pay her to stay and He needed a kidney! After, he explained about what test she would be taking. She was wanting to give him the kidney but before she said "yes," she would have to speak with her mom and family. She had been lied to and all she could do was cry. She needs to hear her mom's side of the story. He tells her he owns hotels, he even had international hotels. She was lost and she asked him, "If she could get back with him, she needed rest because it's a lot. Still no reply to messages or calls she was in deep thought. The gentleman called to take her on a date, and she told him what's going on. She feels close and open to him. But she found out he was sent by her father. Still not knowing how to feel, it's all a set up. Lost and feeling used she could not stomach the pain. She asked, "If they could talk later." But not looking forward to calling him back.

Chapter 9 = Leave or Stay

Can she just feel something real? Can she wake up from this dream? How did all this fall in place like it did? Why do people always need me? They use me up so, I bet when I give this Kidney, he will stop talking to me. The gentleman will be done being fake and using her father's money. But there she goes assuming stuff. There she goes with the negative energy but, How can I be normal in my situation? The trust that she almost had was lost. She believes everyone has wrong intentions. She thinks no one is right. "WELL NOBODY IS RIGHT!" Why is it always like this she thought to herself? "Why do I have to learn lessons with every decision I make?" She then stops to think about Earl. It seems like everytime she would feel like this he will be there changing the subject. But at this moment she is alone. He had to still be at the jail, she called there and he needed to be bonded out. That was what was familiar to her. She decided to have a talk with him before she bonded him out. She had already prepared a flight for him to go back home. But, she didn't know if she was leaving or not but had to get Earl released. He went back home after she bonded him out no problems. He just held his word and left in peace. She knew she needed to close all these chapters in her life. Still missing calls and text messages, she decided to book a hotel that her father didn't own; she needed to get away again. Well she thought he didn't own it. She stayed up late , She knew that with everything on her mind she would not rest. Back with no sleep she decided the next day to not run any more . "Hell, She should be out of breath." She reaches out to her mom and gets understanding before she goes back to talk with her father or the gentleman. At this point she's staying another night.

Chapter 10= The Talk With Mother And Her Siblings

Not only did she need to talk with mom but all her siblings. She was the baby child so everyone should be in one room. She asked everyone to join in on the call. She starts off," Hello, Sorry I haven't been in touch with the family but, we need to talk." They respond, "Spit it out." She answers, "Well the man y'all said was dead, and He has risen!" "Let's call him Lazares"Her brother screams, "Why are you speaking in riddles?" She replied, "On the search to find me, I found a piece I was missing." Her mom replied, "Go ahead, child". She replied, "I found my father and I'm giving him a Kidney, So if you don't hear from me that's why." Her mom said, "What Jessica?" She felt acknowledgement from her family. She wasn't attention seeking but overfilled with the joy of being known. She replied back to her mom, "Yes, mom, a whole kidney for pops." Jessica smiling from ear to ear. "It's not a joke Jessica." She stopped smiling, looking very serious. She looks into the camera, "As if I had a heart attack!" They demanded she come home. They wanted to know where she was. What was she doing? They are ready to go get Jessica but she refuses to give any information but she does share a picture to them. The picture was Jessica holding her dad Jimmy hand, while him receiving plasma. At this time they were all mad. All upset about Jessica's decisions. But, how can they be mad Jessica thought to herself. You don't care for real, you just care because you can no longer use a lie to keep me from my peace.

She felt betrayed because at this point they were still saying your dad died in a fire. The article that is framed in your room tells you that. The names on the birth certificate match. "It is made to look like it is true." Her dad died saving her from a fire because he pushed Jessica out the house far enough from him only he suffered the collapse of the home. They still look at the picture, nobody's face is on the camera, it's all blank but the phone is still connected." Maybe they thought he died and he didn't. "Still no sound from sister or brothers, Jessica spoke, "I'll call you back ". They all got back on the phone and they stressed to her not to do it. They wanted to know where she was. But since 9 she has never been on her family phone bill so they couldn't legally track her. She had everything in her name so, legally she felt she couldn't get tracked. "But didn't Earl find Jessica?" The call finally ended. Days went on with lost communication, it was as if the word was a spreader. Jessica became depressed and she didn't want to do anything. But she thought, "Maybe I'll go to the doctor because I got an Ideal.

Chapter 11 =The Gentleman Waited in the Lobby Till Breakfast was served

"Hello sir, Can I help you." "No! Is it breakfast time yet? Have y'all made the wake up call?" As he was asking questions, there Jessica was. Finally she have left her room. Leaving the front desk he stops Jessica. Jessica and Jim talk. Then here comes K. "I guess he's not a gentleman no more!" She starts to speed back in the elevator. But just in time like a gentleman he stops the door and squeezes right in. "Push your way in why don't you?" Jessica is just freaked out at this point. At this point she is running into a lot of new things that are blowing her mind. "Now you going back to the suite?" He starts off, "Jessica, Can I tell you everything and we can start fresh." She cuts him down, she really is not trying to hear what he is saying but she is scared that if she gets off, he'll try to push himself in a door. She stops and says," Yes K". His name was too long; she didn't even Bother to say it. His name Kwame'Shante He explains everything. He even told her about how and why her room was trashed. Her room was trashed because her dad thought she may have done something crazy like find out who he was. "But they had Earl on the camera! He was in jail!"-- Then K continued, "It was Jim that trashed your room, He thought you had left for good. So we had to track you down with your rental car. After it was confirmed you were on the boat that's when they had met. That's why he ended the call to let Jim know that you have arrived. We tried tracking your phone but, it kept saying you were in your room and the cameras in the hotel said, "You never returned." He got worried, he wished you found out by him. But, he then learned you were enjoying your time on vacation." K decided not to follow up for a few hours." She was amazed at this point. She wanted to know a little bit more about the breakfast man Jim. "Why won't he just go buy a kidney if he can locate things, have him locate a kidney." They decided to forgive and forget and manage a relationship as time went by she went to check on her Jim.

Chapter 12 = The Talk with Breakfast Man Dad

Jessica had an ideal. She thought long and hard. She thought she came up with the best plan. She decided to give Jim her plasma. The doctor arranged a transplant. Her dad was excited. Time went past and Jessica found out some news. She wanted to tell her dad. Weeks later, Jessica was just denied as a plasma donor. This was the first time this had happened after giving plasma. Her blood work came back as a positive test result. She needed to let him know but she wanted to wait. Because she knew that Earl is the only man that could have given her a baby. She explains," Earl was her one and only." He asked," Jessica can you come back tomorrow I'm exhausted? "But, check your account tomorrow, we have to ensure everything is in order." She leaves feeling rejected and disappointed. The next person she had to tell was K. She was nervous but she knew it had to happen. Her family back home was disappointed and she couldn't have more rejection in her life for one day. Jessica decided to go to her room to nap. She fell into a deep sleep. Dreaming of a better outcome. She could not be depressed at this point. "Goodnight!"

Chapter 13 =Bank Transfer

Jessica woke up with 20 million dollars in her bank account. She quickly put on clothes to talk to her dad. "This man is crazy!" She screams. Rushing to her dad Ranch, Where his hospital was. She sees her dad with people. Jim introduce everyone. It was a will meeting. He arranges that everything is split between her and K. Jessica is so confused now. Jessica feels like it is too much to join and commit to be with K after the news she has received. She takes her share and gets the paperwork on everything. But the ranch was left for her and K. How will she get out of that? She allows him to have the home, besides that's his home house and he deserved it. But K in return says, "It's yours ,maybe you will have a reason to come stay." Jim explains at the dinner he is going back home. Jessica's eyes just got big because K had already explained the ultimate set up. But, Jessica rather her father in her life other than to have him raise her man to take care of her. But, because of her father's health. She keeps calm and listens. He is leaving to go back home. He can finally leave. Back when Jim was younger the fire was started because it was Jessica's grandfather that started the fire. Jim opened up about everything, Jessica didn't have to hold in anything. Everything was finally out. So she told her dad how grateful she was but, at this time, she will need to go back to her home to think about everything. They all promise to keep in contact. K was excited about his part and he wasn't okay with Jessica leaving. Still not knowing about the baby situation. She told K that she needed a break and she was going to work things out with Earl.

Besides after these three months K decided to not put up a fight and have her way.

Chapter 14 = Jessica got a baby

It's the one she cares for is the one that she has the most feelings for. "Slow your roll, it almost happened." It's like the second time she almost murmured those words. I want to say," I love you but you are a stranger. She feels as if she says it, it may be too soon. He will reply, "Why do you love me?" Then she said, "She will be scared to open up because she doesn't want to feel rejected. She feels he has more secrets but so does she. She has walls built up from pain. "It's too much, not all in one day", she says. But if not today then when! Time will only tell but she feels as if she's running out of time. But she's done! But are they done? She wondered, "If she will ever live this hard ache again. She's scared so instead of being open she rather let it all rest. Scared to say the news from the doctor. But she doesn't know that he will ask her on the date. She decided to call and ask him to come to her. "MOODY!" She's in pain, she just doesn't want it to stop. But they have only known each other for 3 months. She feels connected to him, she liked him when she didn't even know his name. He let her be free and still made her feel like she was the only one. She forgave him. As time goes by, they finally meet up. "How can I tell him that I'm pregnant?" She wonders if he will ask how the appointment went. She wants to tell him but his eyes are red. There is something wrong. He says, "Can I be Open?" She looks up, "Yes please, I Love you!" He looks at her, "I love you too but our love has been planned for years." She says, "Elaborate!" He looks at her and says, "All my life I was trained to know your love and find the things you love in me." "Your dad is my dad." Jessica says, "Wait you are my bro?" She wondered why no one said anything and is that why Jim did what he did? He says, "Not genetically." Jessica says," Then how?" He says, "My mom kidnapped our dad and nursed him back to health, your dad appreciated my mom. He loves how well raised I was and by 13, I came to him to take a girl on a date. He explained to me the importance of keeping myself ready to be a king. You are a queen!" "We need you to grab the throne with me by your side." Jessica looked up at him and said, "Are you a Virgin, if not you playing and I don't know how to react. He stops her and says, "You must not tell father, I told you because he is sicker than he has led on to have you believe. He also stopped his treatment because this has been stressing us out. "Really he stopped treatment because Jessica was pregnant? Is that why he had to leave?" She needed time to think after the conversation. Jessica stayed and they talked but she had to go back to being alone because it was all too much. So she decided to cut them off and be with her child's father Earl. That was less complicated. But, it turned out to be more drama. He wanted her to kill the unborn. "MY BODY!" Nobody knows what's going on but the doctor and Jessica. Now that she has told Earl and didn't get the response she was looking for she feels rejected even more. Now she feels depressed but,"Earl said he is coming to take her to get rid of the pregnancy.

Chapter 15 = Earl Back

Knocking Loud woke Jessica up. She knew who it was at her door. She hesitated to open the door but Earl Knock got louder. She came to the door he rushed in, he pulled a gun and said, "You will get rid of this baby. Jessica didn't want the baby but at that moment she did. It was just because she hated feeling controlled by a man. So she decided instantly to get in defense mode. Jessica grabbed the phone and ran to the door, he put the gun up to get the phone. Jessica got him close enough to the front door and she threw him out and quickly locked the door. Earl stood at the door apologizing, explaining how sorry he was. Jessica opened the door because she wanted to tell him that at this moment she was keeping the baby. They talked and she said, "She would be coming home, but not to live with him. Jessica was going back to her mom's house with her siblings because at-least she will feel protected, so she didn't want to live alone. I guess it's not all good being alone. Jessica decided to keep what happened to herself. It really bothered her. But, that night she asked Earl to leave. Feeling guilty he left, the tears kept going but at that moment she knew her blood pressure was high but she tried to remain calm. All she could think about K. She wished she had told him how she felt. She wanted to love him and she wanted to be with him and she wanted to tell him she wanted to be with him. "That forever isn't enough." She cried more and more because she was so scared to express them to him. Is it because she is pregnant with another man's baby? Jessica just doesn't want to feel rejected, especially not by love. It was the man she actually liked. It was their conversation, the energy that they had together was unmatched. He made her feel secure. She really believed K. She never felt so comfortable. She loved how he made her feel as if he was trained to respect and honor her. She loved the way she could ask questions and not be afraid. Jessica started to even answer questions. Even if she can't tell him, can she at least tell him she is leaving again. Another knock on the door, she yelled, "Go away!" K said, "But why, we never finished." She came to the door and tried to fix herself before opening the door, K asked Jessica, "Are you okay?" She looked, Jessica said "I'm leaving out tomorrow it was nice to meet you." K looked at Jessica, "I Love you goodbye." Jessica didn't know how to react. He literally took the words out and said goodbye. As he walked away, she waited until he turned the corner and closed the door. Tears and Tears rolling down Jessica's face. She has faced two times where she could have let him know everything and let him make the decision. But his love wasn't strong enough to make her stay. Also the love was not deep enough to share her whole feelings. This was the one time she felt she couldn't talk to K.

Chapter 16= Return to Home for three days

Jessica woke up at 3:00 in the morning. She started packing, She went to the door and it was a knock. It was breakfast delivered, flowers, Visa gift cards, and a road kit. It was all signed by K. She was happy but, yet she decided to make a call to K But, Jessica texted K instead. "Thanks, I'm heading home, talk to you soon." She decided to block K after the text message. She left, she had thoughts of leaving and never coming back. But continued to stay in touch with her dad and he left her the ranch and many assets to own. She knew she would be back but not as soon as anyone could expect. Jessica gets home safe with no problems and her family comes with open arms. Her mom had already cleaned a room out for her and they had an additional room already set up for the lil baby. With so much going on she forgot that she told them everything. They all had to leave an hour early for work due to traffic. They all went to work, she figured they would at least stay the first day. But Jessica had to remember not everything revolves around her. She decided to clean up around the house. A knock came at the door. It was Earl and she wasn't expecting him. She had wished K had come through to talk to her. But, she had already blocked him so why would he just come. She let Earl in, "We are only co-parenting, and we aren't together." Jessica said to Earl at the door. Earl replied, "Whatever we are together, we must raise the baby as a family, I will change." Jessica just allowed to listen to Earl because he will soon have to be at work as well. Jessica told Earl that "she will try", she never said, "yes". But, she never said ,"no"! So to keep everything from going crazy she just told him what she thought he wanted to hear. "But that's not always good!"

Chapter 17= Day 1 At Home

Still Still trying to find peace. She tries the family thing but no matter what Earl does, Jessica is not happy. She is dealing with pain, thinking about K. It's only been barely a day since she has not spoken to K since she had asked for her "space" and blocked his number. She had not told him her secrets and the best way to avoid it she left. As a gentleman like K he was patient. Jessica felt out of control. Jessica had got her job working from home, which allowed her to be wherever she wanted to be as long as she was working. Earl decided to take Jessica out to make her feel like he had once made her feel. Earl wasn't dumb he knew she was only with him in the faith to have a family. It was Earl who always fucked everything up. But, this time Jessica was just waiting for something to happen. Earl falls asleep, His phone keeps ringing. Jessica decides to answer it, it's another baby Moma and they are engaged. Jessica was surprised and hurt but overjoyed but, she thought she manifested the energy, So she woke Earl up and he explain," The girl was crazy and she always say she pregnant." They all talked and got to the bottom of everything and Jessica believed Earl she decided to enjoy her time with him. She knew he wasn't shit but she no longer cared. She began to speak highly and encourage him; she even tells him, "People will come out of nowhere but won't nobody steal our family." At this time Earl really felt love but Jessica didn't feel the same way. Instead of talking about her feelings she pretends to be okay in the name of her family. Jessica was ready to go to bed and wait till 6 in the morning for Earl to leave for work. There was a time Jessica loved Earl's company. She wanted him but he did her any kind of way. He has given himself to all these women with no attachment so she figures she can forgive. "Baby Moms" But, if he knew after Day 3 when she met K she felt something she never felt before. She was in love with a stranger. Earl did not want these types of problems. She felt her feelings could be pushed back because he is just giving dick "FAMILY" but she has given her heart to another man. She knows that was something Earl always gives up on. She played and he tried! But Earl always has something he's up to. But, curiosity drives her insane so she's in love with her mystery man. All she could do is think about K. But she goes to sleep next to Earl but dreams about K as her eyes close. "For the family, for the family, she goes to sleep 'until tomorrow" she says. But, Then she thinks, "I love him not him, I shouldn't be here, I'm not being true to herself.,Should I tell him I don't know who the father is?" Then, Earl would be mad but he would also be gone. But that's not fair!" Jessica finds herself surrounded by lies.

Chapter 18 =Day 2 back Home

Knock at Jessica mom's house. She is the only one there, Earl has left for work. Jessica figures that Earl must have forgotten his lunch. Jessica open the door to yet the biggest surprise of her day's home. It was K standing at the door. Jessica should not be cheesing this hard. She was feeling bad because she was supposed to be stuck with the "Family" but that's not where she wanted to be. She quickly took the smile off her face. She was happy she couldn't hold the mug any longer. She shouted, "I miss you," K said, "Why are you so loud?" Jessica say," I love you, can we leave and I'll tell you everything." K said, "Jessica you no longer have to give your father plasma because we both have donated enough for him, and what he need extra, I will donate to him." She looks up, tears came rolling down her face, "Thank you but, I can't give plasma because, I'm pregnant. I'm not sure why the doctor told you to let me know that but, I'm sorry. He said, "You don't have to be sorry, I forgive you, we all make mistakes." She looked at him like he was crazy. She never heard these words. It's like it is the end of the world. That was another reason why she loved him, it seems like no matter what she thrown at him, he never judged her. He was holding her, she asked, "Could he take her away." Without any hesitation ,everything was packed. As they were leaving she explain everything to her mom and her siblings. Jessica family just wants her to be safe and happy. They encourage her to stay but she was grown. As she was leaving she still wouldn't block Earl but she unblocked K. Jessica didn't last two days home. She was on the way back to her new home. She felt accepted! K asked her," If he can stay over the night because he didn't want to have another night without her. Jessica just wanted to just............... she asked, "If he could come get her in the morning and they could go for Breakfast. As a gentleman like K was, He left and was ready to return the next morning. After K left, Jessica's phone remained to go off and it was Earl she finally told him, "You can be a father to your child, but there is no you and I so let me breathe!" Because she couldn't escape everything. She knew in her mind K was the right choice and she was standing on her truths

Chapter 19=Day 3 Back home

Well the third day never happened. Because she decided to have a new start with K. But as promised they would spend the next morning together. They went out and K surprised her in his private Jet to another country. When she got to the country she was so confused. But she trusted him so she felt safe. They ended up staying out of the country for a while. Little did she know she was going to have a surprise with their whole family. K looked at Jessica, "this is ours! This land has been passed down throughout the generations." They were the longest living family that owned the whole country. Jessica felt like she was in paradise. She had her new family with her and she had a Kwame'Shante. That night was like no other, K got down on his knees at the family ball. He asked Jessica to marry him. Jessica said, "yes" with no hesitation. Although it hasn't been long since they knew each other she felt like he knew her and they had known each other all her life. She was so overjoyed, Jessica would've gotten married right then, but something stopped her. So the family ball was an engagement party that turned into a wedding ceremony. But she wanted to have her baby and she wanted to plan the wedding. She asked K for a month. She would be able to plan everything out and she would be able to have her dream wedding. That's all she ever wanted was to be happy, have generational wealth and a large family. She only thought that all her kids would be from the same man but the plans had left. Jessica always planned her life out. She always wrote down how she wanted Earl to be this ideal man but K was everything that she needed. She thought she was dreaming. She knew her and K had a connection but didn't know he was ready to commit at this age they were so young. K with no kids and about to help raise another man baby without any judgment she was in love. Because to love her, he must love her unborn. She just thought it would be a problem later. The real reason she wanted a month was because that would give K in her mind to show his truths. If he was a monster or if he wasn't a monster she would know in a month's time because they have already gotten to know each other. Now they were living together. But still they haven't been intimate yet because he is patient. "I told yall K was patient!" She was willing to wait until they get married but she thought maybe two months then she would have the baby and be able to heal and recover properly and it would be less stressful on them, but she didn't know how to explain this to K. Because he may think that Jessica is holding back and that could change everything. But then she received a phone call so she needed to leave and go back to her new home. There was a fire at a hotel. She asked K to stay and send for her in two weeks and she would be back. She had to take care of the fire. K said," In two weeks I will have my jet come and get you, be safe, and I love you." She left and this was her first time being on a jet alone. Not only that she had to leave someone she didn't want to leave.

Chapter 20= On the way back home Jessica received good news

On the way back home to the hotel, she receives a phone call and they have found a man that has set the hotel on fire. They were able to put the fire out and it was only the Lovers Room that was burnt. She was also told that a man has confessed and it was an accident and a police report has been written for her insurance claim. She was glad it wasn't Earl because he is always doing something out of anger. She was so happy to be able to call K and let him know it was an accident and everything has been investigated. She asked him, "She should bring some stuff back to Land". Because the country that they had had a private Island that was just for Jessica and K. K of course said, "yes." With no hesitation, you could hear the excitement and she knew she didn't have to call the family because they would soon know because K was so attached to the family. It was as if he really didn't have his own father or family. It was like they all loved K as if he was theirs. Jessica's mom didn't like Earl but accepted him because that's who Jessica was in love with. Jessica's dad didn't even give Earl a chance; it was as if he already had his mind set on K with Jessica only. When she got back to her room she organized and packed all her belongings. She had her outfits out that she was wearing while she was at the hotel; everything out. It was as if she was ready for these two weeks to be over. She was so happy to have Her baby, Family , and K a million miles away that she can trust he's not doing anything sneaky! He had her heart and she had his heart. She wanted this feeling to last forever. She never was able to be and not be in her feelings. K made her feel secure. He was secure as well. He was confident another could not even come close to talking to Jessica or getting her attention. She only had eyes for K and the feelings was mutual. She never been in a mutual relationship, she always felt like she was the only one doing everything to make the relationship last. It's like fresh air when she is with K. Even the sound of his voice makes her still get butterflies, He's still a gentleman, it's like he never changed up the love only begin to get deeper and stronger.

Chapter 21= There is a God

Jessica just received a phone call from the doctor. It is the same doctor that took her and K plasma. The doctor said she just looked over her dad's new blood work and he has been healed. She was so excited she was so ready to get to Jim. She didn't know.

She was happy because now K doesn't have to give anymore plasma and never does. It was like another fresh start. Jessica had been praying for her father to heal. The higher father has healed him. She was so ready to get back and she knew her mom would be happy. The whole time Jessica mom thought no one knew what was going on between her mother and father. But the little girl in Jessica just wanted her mother and father back together. It was like a dream to come true. Jessica siblings will be happy they would feast Jessica!. God is good all the time! Jessica then noticed she needed to pray for what she wanted. She doesn't need to only pray for true forgiveness, pain, and hurt. She could pray through the good times, and the bad times. She noticed she received more blessings when she prayed. Jessica was growing up and she wasn't depressed. It was God who picked her up. Back on an emotional roller coaster , She was always so sad now, Jessica walks around smiling from ear to ear. She has no room for stress. Her father, mother, and siblings were all together in one spot. She decided to make a doctor's appointment with the doctor to make sure her baby was still healthy and fine. The baby was healthy and fine but the due date kind of threw Jessica off. She thought it was another day her baby should be born. But, the doctor told her it's a process then you are pregnant. Jessica believed the doctor this was her first baby and she was just blessed and she felt loved and she felt the love for her baby. It was a feeling like no other. She has never felt the kind of love. She started to plan. She decided to write everything down from the time they met until now and she was going to give him a book when they got married. K would know everything, even the feelings that she hadn't told him about when they first met. It was forever before she could tell him, "I Love You." It was like all the feelings and emotions she felt. No longer did she feel it was fake. She knew K was real and she was ready to get back to the real deal she missed him like crazy. Instead of thinking about crazy insecure things. She only thought positive about K. He could be the one? He is the one! The love they share is unmatched and beautiful. It's a love like no other, it's no judgment, it's all love and she can tell him anything and she always wanted to be open and secure with one person. It was all her prayers being answered.

Chapter 22= Jessica moves to an Island with her family

Jessica couldn't stop thinking about the blessing and she just had to go back to the Land. She missed her family and her boo. She had to leave early, she called K and asked, "If he could send the jet ,she was ready to go. The hotel business had been secured and all her business had been handled so she was ready to leave. Bags had been getting packed since her second day upon arrival. All the business was good she even checked on the other properties her boo and family had. Everything was going good. She felt like her baby will be born in love. Jessica felt that's all she ever wanted as a child. She was so happy. She just didn't know how Earl?. But she didn't say that too loudly, she wanted to continue to be happy. She let Earl know where she would be and K was already informed, the baby was coming so she didn't want to leave Earl out the birth. She knew she would never forgive herself and she didn't want to take that from Earl. But she wasn't going to make it easy. He had to get a passport and have everything together before the baby come because he was allowed to be on the Land for a month after the baby was born. Jessica knew Earl couldn't just pop up in another country. But Earl was better now he agreed to Jessica terms and conditions but he said, " A month is not long enough. As long as I'm only there for my child, I can stay as long as I want." She agreed because Jessica was passive aggressive she just wanted it all to end. She knew she had to take this news back to K. She tell K the conversation between her and Earl and K said, "As long as he don't bother you or try you, He can be there for his child." Again it was rosy red cheeks.

K was the only man that could make her blush, she just only wanted to be with him and that's it. No other man has been able to wear the pants but K was the one. It was as if he was the gentleman that don't seems real. He accepts me and no Judgment. "I hope it stays like this forever," Jessica said. She loved K more and more the days didn't last long enough for their love. Time could stop and it still wouldn't be enough, she would want forever. She would not lose him, and He wouldn't let her lose her. He was truly the man of her dreams. But a part of her just was lost for words. She still gets nervous but never too nervous to let a day go by without telling him that she loved him always and forever. He was an answered prayer she thought.

Chapter 23= The uproar

Earl came early. His passport was rapid, Jessica didn't think he would act that fast. Everyone didn't like that he was there. They very much made him feel uncomfortable. But, K was a gentleman. He treated Earl with respect and gave him access to the hotel near their palace. It was K that made Jessica know everything would be okay. Jessica was getting ready for the baby shower that they were throwing her. She didn't know what she would wear but K had a theme. He brought everyone with a custom . Even one for Earl everything was good until the parents got drunk off wine. Jessica's mom and dad really attacked Earl. They made him so small, Nothing K could do to diffuse this. Everyone is yelling. Nobody's listening; it's like everything is falling apart. Nobody wants to grow up. Earl yell," Fuck all y'all I'm only here for my child. Jessica's mother and father look at each other with laughter. Earl says, "I don't see shit funny!" At this time everyone else is confused but Jessica's parents. So K said, "Y'all are being rude. "What's funny?" Mom and Dad are still quiet and acting like they hear nothing. K asked again. They looked up and said the baby is not yours and they walked away vastly. Jessica was hurt. How could her parents say something like that and then walk off. She couldn't find her mom and dad afterwards. K took her back to the Island and comfort Jessica made her not think about what had just happened. Jessica rested on K chest and slept until the next morning where a repeated phone call woke her up. She had just seen the doctor and she just couldn't take any more bad news so she didn't answer and she held on to K tighter. It woke K up and he held her and let her know everything would be okay and if she answered he would stay there and hold her.

Chapter 24 The call from the doctor

Finally K talked Jessica into answering the phone. Failed payment, no contact Jessica received a call. Sense Jessica has moved to the Land with her family. Everyone in the family has claimed their own zone. Very populated it's hard to manage so many people without a formal government. They really do everything the way the family wants. But they have neglected to reach out to the doctor. She has received failed payment from the last 6 months and she is upset. She states," The baby is K, I injected his sperm at 8 months, when you were supposed to be giving plasma. That is why we always put you asleep in-order to do plasma.And y'all come give plasma together." Jessica's mind is blown and she is sad the whole time she has been believing that it's her fault that her family was not together when she left Earl. But it was another betrayal that was happening. Although the doctor only called because she wasn't getting paid. We had medical attention 8 hours a day. There would always be a nurse by Jessica's side. She really felt like she was royalty. Now she wants to leave but so overjoyed she misplaced her passport a while ago. The sad part about it all because her siblings and mother were on the Land with her. Who did she really have to run to? This time she must face reality and call a meeting. She just wants to be alone but since everything has happened and she was in love. She asked the doctor was "K a part of it all?" The doctor never answered just hung up the phone with, "I need my money!"

Quickly she reached out to the entire family and asked that everyone come to the meeting and this could not wait. She felt played again, what if my whole family knows about this and she is the only one without direction. She continues to wait and everyone arrives. She explained everything that was told to her. In the midst of it all Earl came in unexpectedly and said," I told you!" Jessica tries to run off in tears and her water breaks. K rushed to her and the siblings had to stop the fight between Earl and K and they screamed "Earl leave". Jessica says, "No he's staying until I get a DNA test, He is the only one that's neutral and I only want to be near the better evil." Not thinking what she is saying they all give her what she wishes for.

Chapter 25 The Baby

The baby was a surprise to everyone. "Push Jesse Push," The family yelled! Earl and K both cry because they feel like they are both in a position. Earl feels like it should be his baby and that's how it should be. Earl wants Jessica in his life and he would rather die than have to be away from Jessica and the baby. He knows her! He said he changed! He knows the baby is his. Finally she is here! This was a beautiful baby. Something that she had never seen, it was a baby she envisioned and the baby came true. The baby had light thick brown curly hair with light brown eyes, and big. Jessica named the baby Eiyah'. Jessica thought she had the prettiest little girl. It was a heart melt. She wouldn't put her baby down. Earl was looking at the baby confused; he instantly wanted a DNA Test for everyone. The baby didn't look like K nor Earl. Trying to not think about the doctor. She agreed to the DNA TEST. She wouldn't let K sign the birth certificate. It was going to take three days for Eiyah'. Jessica was so hurt and felt betrayed but every time she looked at her baby she was overjoyed. The baby brought her happiness back. Still the family and Earl were fussing. Jessica machine went off, everyone was escorted out the room. It was Jessica's blood pressure. She had pressure from everyone she asked to be alone the next day. She allowed the baby to be in the glass room that allowed the family and Earl to still be able to see Eiyah' but no access to Jessica. She didn't even want her siblings in the room. She really needed a mental health day. She only wanted her baby and herself to be alone. But she refused to let her feelings get in the way when it came to Eiyah'. So overwhelmed Jessica fell into a deep sleep.

Chapter 26 Together forever

It was the third day. Test results were in and Jessica was ready to let everyone in the room. Jessica had tears in her eyes and she started cramping. She was in labor again and she was scared. It was nothing the doctors could explain. Jessica had siblings three years apart. The Three day baby had blond hair and gray eyes and was small. She named him Eljuh. The babies were different at that time she knew in her head what happened. After she got pregnant with Earl's baby the doctor must have gotten her pregnant again. It was never done before. Jessica didn't want to press charges against the doctor, she started feeling like it was a miracle. Jessica was closer to thirty than 18 so she felt old. She wanted 20 children. With joy her first words after the three day baby was born, she looked up and said,"2 down 18 more to go." They all laughed but she felt like she was with her family, K, and Earl together forever. Earl asked, "If he could take the baby back home with him to be around his family." They all shot it down! Although they aren't twins, siblings must stay together. So they came up with a plan to send the jet once a month to spend time with his child. But Earl came and spent time with both kids, because he wanted to keep the sibling bond. Earl gave them no problems. Earl seemed as if he was changing but Jessica knew he would be up to no good soon. It's like she had no hope for Earl, But for K they decided to live together and co-parent. The wedding was held off until they could find a place as they were before. Jessica didn't want to give up on K, She had a baby from him and she was comfortable where she was. So when she went to check on the hotels and business, Jessica and K always traveled back and forth with the kids. They would even call Earl to invite him. Sometimes he came, sometimes he wanted the girls over for the night. Jessica allowed it because he would always bring his mom when they met up and when he dropped them off. Everything was going smoothly. Jessica asked God for a family and a father that loved her child. Little did she know he would overflow her with two loving fathers? Jessica was still dealing with her trauma and she said, "We all need to be forgiven and they all forgave each other and she prays the peace continues.

Chapter 27 What you going to do?

Time went by and Jessica decided to marry K. It was going to happen and when it did no one would be surprised. Even Earl would be happy! They all became one happy family. The family was finally getting along. The girls were growing up. Everything was as Jessica expected. The intimacy had never started with Jessica and K but the night of the wedding would change that. It was over time to be intimate. The wait was what she loved the most; it was as if he really knew what he wanted. Jessica was nervous and she thought she was moving fast. I guess that's what you could call cold feet. It's like all her sad and depressed feelings came back as if she was making a mistake. But Jessica felt like her time was whining down and she didn't want to have any kids after a certain age. She still wanted to travel but she was wealthy enough to always take her family. She felt like she never had any alone time. She was really overwhelmed but was faking it to make it work. She cried so hard and she was deciding to go through with the wedding but she prayed to make sure she was making the right decision. She still wasn't confident. But , If Jessica wasn't sure of anything, she knew it was the love K had for her and the love she had for K. The day and time have come now she must get it together and grab her father. The bell rings and Jessica is standing at the door. Ready to walk down the aisle to her dream wedding song. To be continued on the day of the Wedding. To be continued…….

Dedication

My Brothers,
My Sisters
My Mom
My Grandmother
Uncle Dre'
Aunties
God Son
Niece
Nephews

Sneak Peak Of Jessica Book 2 Chapter 1

Chapter 1 = Walking Down The Aisle

Jessica was getting ready to walk down the aisle. She thought to herself ,"I hope it all goes a plan." The first door opened up. Jessica walks inside of the first entrance leaving it open ,so her dress would maintain the long look. As the second door is opening, Jessica is nervous. As she was walking , She heard loud music that sounded out her entrance into the wedding. As the door was half way open , She asked for water, But it was from a strange face. Not thinking anything of it she takes the water. She tries to quickly drink it because she doesn't want the doors to open on her wedding day and she was thirsty. The door opened and Jessica was snatched up from her wedding. The doors instantly closed back. The groom rushed down the aisle and by the time he was outside the second door Jessica was gone. Stressing and extremely scared because Jessica doesn't know what's going on. But She tries to cheer up. She tells herself maybe this is a sign. But she thought she deserved to be happy and married. She couldn't stop thinking, She was in the back of the trunk tied up. She remembered that she brought a small gun to keep on her at her wedding. The gun was the same color and design of her dress. She even had real Diamonds on the gun that spelled out her name JESSICA. So started to form a plan in her head. But she needed to break away from being tied up. So in Jessica's head , her plan was made up. Her plan was to find a way to get untied. Then after she became untied, She would shoot the first person she saw. But she also had to be mindful of her bullets; she only had five. Hours went by Jessica still in the trunk she couldn't get her hands untied. Minutes passed by and she felt something sharp poking her. She moved up as far as she could. Moving up and down , Jessica was finally able to break *away from being tied up. She instantly pulled out her gun and now she was ready. 15 minutes passed by and they were at a stopping point. Jessica hears people talking outside the trunk but, she couldn't make out what they were saying. They come open the trunk. First shot went through the first woman arm. Jessica gets out and demand," The keys to the car or She will take the keys because she doesn't know why she has been taken on her wedding day. A girl running up screaming,"Moma ! " Jessica replied , " I need to leave "," I don't have any idea where I'm at or who you are" The girl introduced herself as Ashley. She had been watching Jessica since she found out about the engagement of the wedding. Jessica looks at them and say,"As I have said before please let me leave , For your safety. It's still time for you to take your Momma to a doctor." Ashley looks up and beg ,"Jessica to please look at something." As she explaining Jessica hands are out because she wants the keys to the whip. Jessica day had already been ruined and all she wanted to do was leave. But as she looked around, It was familiar to her where she was. Ashley looked up and ask could they talk. But at this point Jessica would have like too had this conversation versus being taken without her permission on her wedding day. Besides if Ashley was seeing and spying on her, Why couldn't she have approached Jessica? Still looking lost, Jessica asks again ," Give me your keys and I'm leaving. Instantly she comes at Jessica ," Screaming look don't shoot!" Jessica stopped her instantly. Ashley was losing time and wasting Jessica time. So Jessica reached down and grab the keys. She tell her ,"Don't Fuck with me Crazy Ass ,I'm leaving. As Jessica leaving , Her gun remained pointed , and here pops up K. Jessica is lost. "Why is he here, and is this a set up? She instantly jumps out of the car and walks over to K car. As she walks the gun is still up but now it's on K.*

About Author:

My name is Tempestt Lyles, and I am from Thomasville Georgia. I love to do electrical work, I would like to start playing with the Trumpet, and I love expressing myself through writing. Art surrounds me, and I also enjoy crafting. The next book I will be writing is about what happened to Jessica and her life during the wedding. Stay tuned to the writing.

www.ingramcontent.com/pod-product-compliance
Lightning Source LLC
LaVergne TN
LVHW041544060526
838200LV00037B/1135